EVE BUNTING

Blackbird Singing

DRAWINGS BY STEPHEN GAMMELL

Macmillan Publishing Co., Inc.
New York
Collier Macmillan Publishers
London

To Ron and Jackie Kitchen
and the children of Illiopolis, Illinois.
Thank you for your help with
Blackbird Singing.

Copyright © 1980 Eve Bunting
Copyright © 1980 Macmillan Publishing Co., Inc.

Macmillan Publishing Co., Inc.
866 Third Avenue, New York, N.Y. 10022
Collier Macmillan Canada, Ltd.
Printed in the United States of America
10   9   8   7   6   5   4   3   2   1

LIBRARY OF CONGRESS CATALOGING IN PUBLICATION DATA
Bunting, Anne Eve.
Blackbird singing.
SUMMARY: Pulled apart by his parents' stormy
relationship, which comes to a climax when their crops
are threatened by huge numbers of migrating blackbirds,
10-year-old Marcus struggles to come to terms with himself, his parents, and a complex ecological dilemma.
[1. Birds—Fiction. 2. Ecology—Fiction.
3. Stuttering—Fiction] I. Gammell, Stephen. II. Title.
PZ7.B91527Bn   [Fic]   79-23294   ISBN 0-02-715360-6

1

I stood behind Mom, watching her paint. She had set up her easel in her favorite place, with the house behind her and the stand of trees in front. Fred Johnson, our fat black cat, lay at her feet, his tail moving just enough to make the tasseled grass sway. The smell was horrible here, so close to the foulness of the droppings under the trees.

Mom's picture was only partly finished, and I knew she was waiting for the birds.

Her head tilted back, then swung expectantly toward the west, and I heard them coming, too, heard them before I saw them.

Fred Johnson's tail had come alive now, whipping like a thin, black snake. His ears twitched.

The birds came with the rustle of their own wind, and their voices, all screaming together, bounced off the last of the day. The fish and wildlife man had said there were probably more than a million of them roosting in our trees.

Mom watched without moving as the flock soared under the night clouds, and it was as if all of them were joined together, all those thousands and thousands of birds, grackles and cowbirds and the blackbirds with their scarlet wing patches flashing a bright gleam of color that came and went as they settled themselves into the branches of our maples. They hung there, still screaming their harsh, shrill cries, and the trees bent and swayed and groaned under the burden of the birds.

A mosquito sucked from my arm and I swatted at it.

Mom turned and made a face at me. "Drat," she shouted. "Missed them again." Even shouting it was hard to hear her over the racket the birds made.

I smiled. Mom had been coming out here night after night to catch the birds' homecoming with her watercolors. And each night she sat engrossed, forgetting to paint.

Mom loved the birds the way she loved the trees and music, and everything beautiful. Dad hated them. I thought that they were beautiful, but still, I was afraid of what they were doing to us, and I wanted them to leave, to fly away forever.

"I guess I'm going to have to do them from memory, Marcus," Mom yelled, putting away her paints and standing up. "But how can I remember something as incredible as that?"

She took the picture, and I folded the easel and walked behind her carrying it and the kitchen chair she'd been sitting on.

Fred Johnson padded in front on soundless paws, his jeweled collar sending off sparks green as his eyes. The collar was Mom's idea and was supposed to warn away the birds that Fred Johnson was stalking. But Fred Johnson was too fat to be a threat to anything. Dad was always whispering to Fred to make himself useful and catch a few blackbirds. Fred Johnson tried all right, but fat Fred just wasn't a bird-catching cat.

Night was almost here. I liked the shadowless grays of the late summer nights, with chores done and the dark lying on the fields outside. Inside, the light and the closeness held Mom and Dad and me together. But it was only that way when things were good between them.

I hoped Dad wouldn't be in yet from the milking because if he saw Mom's easel he'd get angry again and say something mean in that hard new voice of his.

It wasn't that he didn't like Mom painting. We had her pictures hung all over our house. Some of mine were framed and hung, too, and Dad was all the time showing them to people and acting proud of us. But he didn't like her painting the birds that were destroying our corn.

Mom pushed open the kitchen door and held it for me so I got inside ahead of her. I stood, blinking in the kitchen light, not wanting to see what I was seeing because I knew it meant more fighting.

Dad was cleaning his second shotgun, the one I always used when we went hunting. His other, newer one leaned against the wall. It was beautiful, too, in its own way, all gleaming metal and warm, rich, polished wood. I carried the chair inside and put it in its place at the table, waiting for Mom to speak.

"Marcus will not go with you in the morning," she said. "I will not allow him to wantonly kill."

I arranged the chair neatly, taking pains to line it up exactly with the other three chairs. I imagined four chalk circles on the floor where the chair legs should be and I jiggled it this way and that, getting it just right. I wouldn't look at Mom. I didn't have to. I heard the shake in her voice and I knew the way her mouth would be.

"Marcus will go," Dad said. The rag made a whispering sound as he pulled it in and out of the gun barrel.

"Run and wash your hands for supper," Mom said to me.

I went upstairs, glad to escape, but I could still hear their voices in the kitchen, and *I* hated the birds. They were eating our corn. Their droppings were inches deep under the trees and the smell came into our house. The birds were pests, vermin. Why had they come and spoiled everything?

The fish and wildlife man said they had stopped here in Erie County on their yearly migration south. But why had they chosen our trees? The bird man had shrugged when we asked. "Maybe they've changed their flight pattern for some reason. This year, you're on it."

I combed my hair, just to kill some time before I went downstairs. I could still hear Mom's and Dad's voices rising and falling as they argued, and, like a background chorus, the screeching and quarreling of the birds. That sound was always there now, except in the daytime when the birds were off foraging. It was the new accompaniment to our lives. That, and the unfriendliness in our house.

Mom and Dad had had differences before. Lots of them. But I couldn't remember the fighting ever lasting this long. Mom didn't like it when Dad killed one of our chickens for the table, and she always took the truck and disappeared on hog-butchering days. Dad and I were the ones who wrapped the meat and packed it in our big freezer, and of course she didn't eat any of the pork, any meat, although she fixed it for us.

"You were never meant to be a farmer's wife, Sabrina," I'd heard Dad say once. "You should still be playing your guitar somewhere, in some fancy night place like Simon's Spot." Simon's Spot was where Dad had first seen Mom, singing her own music, and it was to Simon's that they still went on their anniversaries. But he'd smiled at Mom while he said it and she'd smiled back and wrinkled her nose. Then he'd hugged her hard and there was such a softness in both of them that I'd known he loved her more than anything and that he wouldn't change her, even if he could. But he wanted to change her now.

I couldn't hide upstairs any longer. It was really bad being me these days. Just about as bad as it had been last Christmas, and last Christmas had been the worst. That's when I'd started stuttering and Mom took me to Kelsey's clinic.

Kelsey said the stuttering was a symptom of deep psychological problems. I don't even like to think about Kelsey. Thinking about her's enough to bring the stutters back right now.

Which side am I on anyway? I wondered as I dragged downstairs. Mom's or Dad's? Both? Neither?

We scarcely talked over dinner except to say, "Pass the biscuits," or "Peas, please." Things like that.

After we'd eaten Dad said, "Go on up to bed now, Marcus. I'll be waking you at sunup."

Mom didn't say anything, so I figured Dad had won that round.

I went to my window before I got into bed. Even though it was so hot the window was closed tight because of the smell. Heat lightning flickered far off in the distance.

Across the meadow the blackbirds clumped together on the tree branches. Some flew around still, restless under the pale, crescent moon. From here the trees looked as though they hung heavy with some strange, rich fruit. Shining black eggplant maybe, or giant purple passion plums.

Below me someone opened the door and I saw Dad stride across the meadow, the shotgun barrel catching and reflecting the light of the moon.

I held my breath as he stopped under the trees, and I saw the white blur as he turned his face to the sky.

He raised the gun and the shotgun blast shattered the night. Again and again he reloaded and fired into the trees, and the birds rose in a screeching, splintered cloud, then settled again, jostling for space on the branches.

Dad must have got off a couple of dozen shots.

He looked old as he walked back across the meadow to the house. I stepped away from the window so he wouldn't see me. Poor Dad.

Fred Johnson was curled on my pillow. I got into bed and took him with me and held him close, but through the rumble of his purring I could still hear the ugly, raspy voices of the birds. There was no getting away from them. Poor Dad.

2

Mom served us oatmeal for breakfast. I didn't feel much like eating. The sun was barely up, but the kitchen was hot and sticky already. Good corn-ripening weather.

"You'll drive the truck," Dad said. He was telling Mom, not asking her.

Mom nodded. Her face looked as if someone had siphoned the blood out of it.

Dad and I put on our red nylon jackets. Red was our shooting color. I climbed into the back of the truck and Dad handed up the two guns. He jumped in beside me.

"Be careful, Marcus," Mom said.

"He knows how to handle a gun," Dad said coldly. "He's known how since he was seven years old."

Mom reached up and buttoned one of my buttons that I'd missed. "Be careful, Marcus," she said, just as if Dad hadn't spoken, wasn't even there.

She started the truck so quickly that Dad and I staggered against each other and had to grab hold of the sides to keep from falling.

"She'll kill us before we get there," Dad said, and he tried to grin at me in the old way. But the grin wouldn't have fooled anybody.

I heard the sound of the birds rising from the trees and I tried not to look at them as they flew above us in a jagged, dotted pattern. They were a ballet, moving to music, swift and clean, black and red and shining in their perfection. The birds were beautiful.

"There they go," Dad said. "Another day feeding off us."

When she got on the narrow road that bordered our cornfield Mom slowed the truck. But still the gravel spattered up, coating the legs of our jeans with its white powder.

The birds had gotten here before us.

We saw hundreds of them drop into the green cornstalks, but as soon as they landed they disappeared from sight. To look, after they'd settled, was to see an empty field.

Dad rapped at the cab window and Mom stopped the truck.

We began shooting.

At each shot the birds would rise, slanting up in a broken black line. The trick was to get a hit while one was in the air, before they came down again.

Mostly we missed because the birds were far away and moving, but we did get some of them.

After about ten minutes or so in one place Dad would rap the window and Mom would move us to another part of the field. We kept shooting while the truck moved, and it was fun.

I hit one bird that was flying high, a smaller black one without wing patches that looked like a grackle. It fell, fast and hard as a rock dropped from a bridge.

"Good shot, Marcus," Dad said, and I felt as if I'd never been happier, here with Dad, the gun barrel warm and smooth under my hand, the power that came with holding it.

Mom's head and shoulders suddenly appeared out of the cab window. "Can't you see how crazy this is, Sam?" Her voice shook. "There are close to a million birds in that roost. What good does it do to shoot ten or twenty of them?"

"That's ten or twenty that won't eat our crop," Dad said.

"They'll go soon, Sam. They have to."

"Yeah." Dad reloaded his gun. "They'll go. After they've cleaned out our harvest."

I sighted into the corn and fired.

Suddenly the birds rose together—I guess there were maybe two or three hundred of them—and they flew up in a black shimmer of wings and skimmed away.

"We got 'em," Dad said, and he thumped me on the back. "Now they're somebody else's problem. Stay here," he told me, and he jumped down and walked into the field.

My heart began to thump. Was he going to find and bring back the bird I'd shot—all bloody, maybe without a head or with a hole through its chest? I swallowed. Please, Dad. Please don't. And to myself I said, "I didn't mean to do it. The birds weren't real out there. It was like a game, shooting at a target. Like at the county fair. I'm sorry."

Dad was coming back. I could see the tall green cornstalks rustling, and now and then he'd appear through a space.

He was carrying something.

My stomach lurched, then settled when I saw it was an ear of corn.

He threw it on the front seat next to Mom.

"There's what your blackbirds do. Take a look at

that, eaten halfway down, every kernel punctured. Droppings fouling the silk! We're losing ten percent of our yield per acre to those damn birds."

"You could have scared them away," Mom said. "You didn't have to make Marcus kill them."

"He didn't make me," I said. For a terrible second, as I said that word *make*, I thought my stutter was back. But I replayed the sentence in my head and it sounded all right. Kelsey had said I might get the stutters again, and the blinks too. Well, Kelsey could be wrong about that, like she was wrong about a lot of things.

Mom started the engine the second Dad got into the back of the truck. "Can we go home now?" she asked.

She drove too fast again on the way back and Dad and I were jolted and rattled around on the truck bed.

As we were climbing down Mom said to Dad, "I expect they're back by now, all of them, and the others they've brought along with them, too, all of them eating your precious corn." She pushed her face close to his and there was a terrible, gloating kind of look on it.

"It's your corn too," Dad said. "And Marcus's. And that corn's the money for our winter feed, and for the oil to keep us warm. That corn's our life."

Mom's throat moved as if she was having trouble swallowing. Then she turned and walked into the house and the kitchen door slammed. Mom wanted the birds to go as much as any of us. She didn't want the corn eaten, and Dad worried and mad at everybody all the time. It was just that she couldn't stand to see them killed. Poor Mom.

"Come on, son," Dad said. "The cows and hogs need fed, watered." His hand was warm on my shoulder, and I heard myself creak and crack, not knowing what I believed, and I gathered myself tight inside my skin for protection.

"Those damn birds," I said.

3

Dad got a phone call just after midday dinner. Before he took his cap to go out again he said, "That was Joe Dobbs. He had an agricultural agent up at his place this morning. He's bringing him over here this afternoon."

"What for?" Mom asked.

"It's about the birds," Dad said, and Mom didn't ask anything more.

Joe Dobbs's farm was next to ours and he had the same bird problem we had. Sometimes, when I thought about it, it did seem crazy, like Mom said. Dad would go out in our cornfields a couple of times a day and scare the birds away. Likely he was scaring them straight to Joe Dobbs's corn. And Joe Dobbs and Joe Jr., who was my best friend, and Karl, their hired man, would go out shooting and scare the birds out of their fields back to ours. But what else was there to do? Unless the agricultural agent had something in mind.

I didn't see the agent come because I had gone to the river, the way I did every afternoon when my chores were finished. Me and Joe Jr. and Hubie Keller and three or four of the other kids from the town kept a bunch of old inner tubes stashed under the trees and we roped ourselves together and floated, drinking dented cans of soda pop that Hubie's brother got for three cents each from the market where he worked. He sold them to us for five. As usual, we were talking about the birds. Sometimes I wondered what we'd talked about before the birds came.

"What did the agent say?" I asked Joe Jr.

"He didn't say much because they were in a hurry to get to your place," Joe Jr. said. "But I think the guy's going to fix something up for us."

Hubie snorted. "Fix something up! We've heard that before."

We floated lazily with our faces turned to the heat of the sun and our rear ends and feet cooled off by the river. Now and then a solitary blackbird or a sweep of a dozen or more would wing overhead, flying lazily, like leaves on the wind.

"Too bad the firecrackers didn't work," Joe Jr. said. "But we sure had fun that night."

I scratched my big toe on the joining rope. The firecrackers had been great. All those blue lights and rockets going off in the sky, and the birds screaming their heads off, zooming up, circling around and around, their bodies hidden in darkness, then silhouetted against the dazzling bursts of light, like birds in a scary movie, their necks stretched out, their beaks gaping from the force of their screeching. They'd flown away, and we'd all cheered and clapped each other on the back. I'd seen Mom crying, so I knew she was happy. When she was happy was the only time she cried. When she was sad her face closed up and her mouth got soft and squashy.

But the birds had come back in the night and when we woke in the morning the trees were filled with them again. Dad thought there were even more than before.

"They told their buddies it's the fourth of July around here," he had said grimly. "They've all come back for the next show."

We'd tried the firecrackers three nights in a row.

"There's not a creature alive that's going to stick around where it's not comfortable," Winter Claghorn had said. Winter has a farm farther on down our road. But the blackbirds did.

Another time we'd tried drowning them out.

Dad and a bunch of the men rigged up sprinklers under the roost. We had to give up on that too.

"Them damn birds is enjoying the shower bath," Joe Dobbs had said. "Frisking around there like a mob of kids in a backyard hose. All we're doing's keeping them cool and comfortable."

Like the river was keeping us cool and comfortable now. I moved my rear so the water could slosh over my stomach.

Joe Jr. floated his empty root-beer can downstream

and sighed. "Those firecrackers sure were great though."

I told them about the bird I'd shot that morning.

"Got him clean as a whistle," I said. "I bet I took the head clean off that dirty old bird." There was a flicker of something inside me when I remembered how I'd felt, thinking I'd have to see it, all bloody and messy. But I hadn't had to. So that was all right. "B-b-blew it to b-b-blazes!" I said.

I heard the words, heard my own voice stammering over them, and I couldn't believe it. No! It had to be a mistake. It couldn't be happening again! I bent forward and splashed some of the cold, gray river water that flowed between my bent knees over my face. Had Joe Jr. heard?

He was fishing for another can of pop. We tied the cans to our tubes and let them trail behind us so they'd stay cool. Joe was pulling the tab off with his teeth. Joe's teeth are awfully big, but they are great for opening cans. Mom said his face would grow into his teeth and that when Joe was big his teeth would be just the right size. That had me puzzled. If my teeth stayed the same size they'd be too small for the rest of me. I'd have a mouth like an eel's. As if I didn't have enough to worry about.

Naw! Joe hadn't heard a thing. Maybe I'd imagined the stuttering myself. I'd try another sentence. A hard one. Something with *s*'s. I remembered the last time,

Kelsey leaning toward me in her clinic office and asking, "What are your parents' names, Marcus?"

I'd mumbled something under my breath.

"Speak up." Kelsey getting mad.

"S-s-s-sam," I'd said. "And S-s-s-sabrina."

Kelsey had smiled at Mom then. "See?" she'd said. "See why he has trouble with *s*'s?

It was a bunch of bull. I had trouble with a lot of other letters too. But the *s*'s were the worst.

"Sam and Sabrina," I said now, under my breath. My heart was chug-a-lugging and I felt sweat trickle from under my armpits.

"Sam and Sabrina," I said loudly. There! It had come out perfectly. It was like a good omen, and I beamed my relief on Joe Jr. "It's a code," I said to their startled faces, and I lay back and closed my eyes. Happiness flowed over me with the river water. I was O.K.

We untied our lines then because we were pretty close to where the river ran fast and rough, and the ride was better solo. I lugged my tube back and rode the river again after the others had left. No hurry getting home. It was better here on the river.

4

I passed Ridley Hills on the way back. We came here every spring to hunt for mushrooms and in the fall to gather big, green, prickly horse chestnuts. Ridley Hills has the best blackberry thickets too. We'd come picking here last summer, the three of us. It was around the end of August and the berries were deep purple, bursting with juice. They'd soon be ripe again. I wondered if we'd come this year.

It almost hurt to think about last time. I know when you think back on things they sometimes seem better than they really were. They seem just about perfect and that's not exactly right. But that day we went blackberrying was special. It was the day we saw the unicorn.

Mom always saves the ice-cream cartons for berry-picking, the kind with handles, like little plastic buckets. We'd each brought one. We'd hung them from our belts to leave our hands free and I remember we'd picked all afternoon till our fingers were stained all the way to the knuckles with bright purple juice. I remembered the stickers too, though, so I wasn't making it out to be better than it really had been. You can't get away from being snagged and stuck and poked at and bitten by chiggers when you're blackberrying.

Dad's always the best picker. I eat too many of my berries and Mom's all the time stopping to admire the way a leaf looks or to listen to a bird singing.

When we'd about three quarters filled our buckets and were getting tired we hunched our way out of the brambles and lay in a tufty, lumpy meadow, resting and looking up at the clouds.

Mom might not be the best berry-picker but she sure is the best cloud-watcher. Dad and I can see ordinary cloud pictures, like snowmen or sailing ships. But Mom! Hers are different.

That day, that last blackberrying day, she'd seen a unicorn.

It took Dad and me a while to find it, but Mom said, "Don't you see him there, over on the slopes of that cloud mountain? His mane is blowing and he has his head thrown back smelling the wind? Marcus, look!"

Her head close to mine and her finger pointing. "See his horn, thrusting up into that circle of blue?"

And I looked where her hand traced the shape and there he was, just the way she said, the unicorn, pawing at the clouds that swelled around his little hoofs.

"And look, oh look!" Mom's voice was breathless, filled with wonder. "He's running!"

And he was, scudding along, free and windblown.

"Do you see a castle and is he going to rescue the princess in the tower?" Dad asked teasingly, but his hand was over Mom's and his fingers were twined in hers.

"No. He's running into the woods there. See the woods, Marcus, all fluffy with springtime blossoms? A maiden is there, waiting for him, and he'll come to her and lay his head in her lap."

"And then what?" I asked, because it was all so real, all happening there in the pictures spread out above us. I'd half wanted Joe Jr. to come picking with us today, and having Joe Jr. would have been great too. But he wouldn't have been able to see this. He'd have dragged me off somewhere to look for frogs.

"She came to find him. She knew he'd come because a unicorn always shows himself to those who are self-less and pure of heart," Mom said softly. "She'll ask him to go with her to where her sister lies on a bed of pain. Only the touch of his magic horn can heal her sister's hurt and make her well again."

"Will he go?"

"Of course he'll go."

I was lying there in the hot old field and I could see it all up in the sky. The streaming mane of the unicorn, the long trailing hair of the maiden who rode him, their dream gallop, gliding silently across the cloud-strewn sky.

Mom's hand came out to take mine so the three of us were joined. The chiggers had got to me around the ankles and I wanted to scratch, but I didn't dare break the spell.

"Marcus? Did you know that when Noah put all the animals in the ark at the time of the flood the unicorns were playing and got left behind?" Mom asked. "That's why they are so rare."

I was glad it was Noah's fault. I'd been half-afraid the unicorns were like the buffalos, wiped out by hunters, and thinking about them would make Mom depressed. But it would have been hard for even her to be mad at Noah.

"Are there any unicorns now?" I asked. "Real unicorns?"

Mom smiled. "Didn't one just show himself to us? Lucky people can always find a unicorn in the sky."

I know Dad loved Mom then. And that was only last summer. And he still loved her. He did. He'd told Kelsey that, hadn't he?

I looked up now at the evening sky and shivered. No unicorns. There were a few clouds hazy above Ridley Hills tonight, but nothing that looked a bit like a unicorn—or even a plain old sailing ship. There were two blackbirds though. Sure, I thought. The damn birds drove the unicorns away and our luck right along with them. I hugged my river-wet towel bundle and walked faster.

I stopped at the back porch before I went in the house, and I got the slops and took them out to the hog barn.

The birds weren't back in their trees yet. Maybe Dad would take me shooting again tonight, after we'd eaten. Maybe he was going to take me all the time now.

I pushed open the kitchen door slowly, because I never knew how it would be now when they were together. The kitchen was filled with a sharp, fruit smell.

Mom had fixed blackberry pie. It gave me a jolt to see it on the table since I'd been thinking about last year's blackberrying all the way home. She must have gone by herself today and picked the berries. Heck, they weren't even properly ripe yet. We never took the berries this early. It made me sad to think of her going up to Ridley Hills alone. I wondered if she'd been thinking about last year too. If she'd remembered the unicorn.

Blackberry pie was Dad's favorite. Mom didn't particularly like to bake and I knew she'd done it specially to make up for the way she'd been at the cornfields this morning. Usually, with Mom's pie, Dad would make some remark about how terrific it was, and about how he'd never expected when he married a looker like her that he'd get a gourmet, live-in cook too. But this time he ate Mom's pie as if it were store-bought. It wasn't as sweet as it usually was. It was kind of mouth-puckering and I knew I'd been right about the berries not being ripe. Still, it was good.

I wanted to ask about the agricultural agent, but it wasn't smart to remind them of the birds, so I kept quiet.

We heard them when they came back to their roost. There was no way to miss them with the clatter and chatter they made. Dad had made no move to go shooting tonight and Mom had stayed away from her paints. It was as if there was a bargain between them.

When the blackbird noise came, the sound sweeping into the night's quiet, rising, fading as they wheeled, rising and growing again as they turned, Dad just raised the volume on the 8 o'clock news. The babble of the million bird voices drowned it for a few seconds, the beeping like radar, like bats, like a million Martians. Then we could hear again as the birds settled for sleep.

Dad should have turned the TV off instead of up. There was a story on about an anti-sealing group in Canada. "This past spring 97,000 baby seals were slaughtered in the animal hunt," the TV announcer said. We saw pictures of ice floes, and the baby seals with their pup faces. And we saw the hunters walking over the ice, clubbing the baby seals to death. Then they'd drag the bundles of dead fur over the ice, leaving ribbons of red behind them on the whiteness.

"These people today are trying to convince the prime minister that this kind of hunt should not be allowed to happen again."

Mom didn't say a single word. But she could have been shouting, and her accusations lay there between the three of us. Which was dumb, because I'd never even seen a seal except in the zoo and I sure as heck wouldn't kill one. Dad wouldn't either.

"I guess the sealers have to make a living, same as anybody else," Dad said, and I wished he just hadn't said anything. Those were almost the same words he'd spoken when Mom put her SAVE A PORPOISE, BOYCOTT TUNA sticker on the back of our truck. "Are the tuna fishermen supposed to starve?" he'd asked. Why couldn't he just keep quiet?

It was about an hour later that Dad had another phone call.

When he finished listening, he said something quietly, then hung up.

"Some men are coming over to talk business with me, Sabrina," he said. "They'll be here in a few minutes."

I had the strangest, surest feeling that Dad had been expecting the call and that it had to do with the birds, and whatever was happening was the reason we hadn't gone shooting tonight. There had been no bargain.

Mom cleared away the supper things that were still on the table. She poured the coffee grounds from the pot, and measured in some fresh spoonfuls, and she never once said to Dad, "Who's coming? What are they coming for?" Because she didn't ask I knew that she suspected something, too, and was afraid.

I opened the door to the men when they came. The bird sounds and the birds' smells crowded in with them.

Joe Dobbs came in first, then Winter Claghorn and another man who was a stranger. The stranger wore a short leather jacket and white pants with creases, sharp as the fold in a paper. Under his arm was a plastic folder. His nails were shiny and I could tell right off he wasn't a farmer.

"This here's Flit Crockett," Joe Dobbs said, nodding up at the man in the jacket. "He's the one the agent got for us, Sam."

Dad said, "This is my wife, Sabrina, and my son, Marcus."

Flit Crockett smiled. I could see by the way that he stared at Mom that he was bowled over. People always got that way when they saw her for the first time. Even Joe Jr. says Mom's pretty. He says Hubie's big brother says she has bionic legs. I guess my grandma had great legs, too, when she was young. She was a show girl then. I have a poster of her on my wall. She says the girl primping on it is for sure her, though nobody would know it if she didn't tell. Of course Grandma's pretty old now. She lives in Florida and we don't see her too often. She says Ohio is always either too hot or too cold, and we can't take the time off to go to Florida. You can never take time off when you're a farmer. I have a grandpa too. He's Dad's father. Since he had his stroke he can't walk. He lives in Minnesota with my Aunt Betty. This used to be his farm, and once my Dad was a boy and tagged around behind him the way I tag behind Dad. If Grandpa was here he'd want the birds to go too.

Joe Dobbs and Winter Claghorn and Mr. Crockett sat around the table and Mr. Crockett kept watching Mom as she poured the coffee, as if he was mesmerized. He reminded me of fat Fred Johnson watching his rabbit hole. Fat Fred sat for hours in front of that dumb hole, licking his chops, and Dad said there hadn't been a rabbit near that hole for the last ten years. More like the last twenty.

"Flit's a licensed pest-controller, Sabrina," Joe Dobbs told Mom. "I expect Sam's told you about him."

"No," Mom said. "Sam hasn't told me anything."

"Flies his own plane," Joe Dobbs said. "He's just come up from around Alliance. They have the same trouble with the birds we're having."

"Had," Flit Crockett said. "They had trouble with their birds. But not any more. Know what I mean?"

"Had!" Joe Dobbs chuckled. He had a face like an old withered leaf and eyes that were dark brown with yellow rims. I figured Joe Jr. was pretty lucky not to look like his dad. It must be tough enough having those monster teeth. But they'd probably work out O.K.

Flit Crockett was still staring at Mom. I swear, I saw him run his tongue across his lips just the way Fred Johnson does. "I'm the one's going to get rid of them pesky birds for you, Mrs. Miles," he said.

If he thought Mom was going to throw herself into his lap and kiss him or something he was disappointed.

She raised her eyebrows and said, "Really?" in her most stuck-up voice. Then she asked, "Do you work with seals, too, Mr. Crockett?"

Flit Crockett smiled and asked, "Pardon me?"

"Nothing," Dad said angrily.

Mom set the coffeepot back on the stove, picked up the overalls I'd been asking her to shorten for the past month, got her sewing box and sat away from us under the gooseneck lamp.

I stood behind Dad.

"So how do you do this?" Dad asked. His voice was cold. Mr. Crockett better watch it. Once I'd heard Dad say to a salesman, "I never buy from someone who drools over my wife when he's supposed to be selling to me."

I looked carefully and didn't see any drools on Flit Crockett's lips. But still.

"I'm a bird exterminator," Flit Crockett said. "Poison, sprayed from my plane. Know what I mean?"

"You're going to p-p-poison the b-b-b-birds?" I

asked. And I was stuttering again too. I gripped hard on the back of Dad's chair. How could it be? I'd said the *s*'s O.K. And *s*'s were harder. I glanced quickly at Dad. He didn't seem to have noticed, but Mom's hands had stopped moving. I made myself look at her and she was staring at me, the steel pins she held between her lips shining in the lamplight.

Flit Crockett smiled up at me. He probably thought I talked this way all the time. "That's right, son. We use a poison called Avatril. It's pretty interesting the way it works. We treat some corn chop, about two percent of what we're going to use. Then we spray the chop from my plane onto the cornfields." He rolled his fingers together as if he had a bead between them. "The chop's round, and it rolls right off the corn and lies in the rows. The birds go for it like a kid goes for candy."

"It doesn't hurt the corn?" Winter Claghorn asked.

"Nope," Flit said. "Just rolls right off it. Now, since we only treat two percent of the stuff, that's how many of the birds it kills. But it's what the birds do before they die that's the interesting thing. That Avatril drives them clean out of their heads. They go swooping away up in the air, yelping and crying and doing the craziest stuff. It scares the rest of them out of their wits. They take off like a bunch of jet fighters, and they don't come back. Whatever it is those dying birds yell at the others, it gets rid of them fast. Then you just gather up the dead ones and your problem's over."

Winter Claghorn said, "Show Sam the pictures, Flit. You know what they say. Pictures speak louder than words."

Flit Crockett pushed his coffee cup aside and laid the plastic folder on the table in front of him.

"Come over here, Marcus," Mom said sharply. "I want to see if these overalls are the right length."

I stayed where I was.

"Now," Mom said.

"Dad?" That was what I meant to say, but it came out "D-d-d-dad?"

Dad looked up at me, sort of puzzled, and I wasn't sure still if he'd caught on to the stuttering. Then he looked across at Mom. "Go to your mother, Marcus," he said. I knew he didn't like Mom protecting me from things like pictures of dead birds. But he wouldn't start any hassle in front of the neighbors.

I heard the sound of the zipper on the folder sizzling around as I walked reluctantly to Mom's chair. "Here," she said, holding out the overalls. "Step into them. You don't have to take off your jeans."

Flit was pulling out big shiny photographs and passing them to Dad.

"Look at that one," Winter said. "Look at all them dead birds, Sam."

"What makes their legs turn backward like that, Flit?" Joe Dobbs asked.

I stood as tall as I could while Mom knelt, pinning up the pant legs. But I couldn't see a thing.

"The stuff gets their central nervous system," Flit said. "It's pretty dangerous. I can't do any job without an agricultural agent inspecting and giving me an O.K. Know what I mean? But he's O.K.'d you."

"Two percent," Dad said.

"With what you've got here, that'll give you about twenty thousand dead birds," Flit said.

Joe Dobbs slapped the table. "Twenty thousand. That's better than we can do with the guns, Sam. Sure wish you could get rid of my gophers for me, too, Flit. Those damn gophers are eating up my root crops faster than I can pick them."

"Strychnine's the only thing that'll work with them," Flit said.

Joe Dobbs nodded. "I got me some yesterday."

Winter Claghorn studied a picture. "It's strange the way the black color's bleached right out of some of these birds. They look damn near gray."

Joe Dobbs chuckled. "They aged overnight."

Mom made a little sound like a whimper, and I looked quickly down at her.

She was sitting back on her heels. There was a small drop of blood on her finger where she'd stuck it on one of the pins. The drop was red and shining as the flash on a blackbird's wing.

"You all right, Sabrina?" Dad asked.

Mom stood up, holding onto the back of her chair.

"Excuse me," she said, and she went fast out of the room. I heard the bathroom door slam.

As soon as she'd gone I dashed across to the table and riffled through the pictures, tripping over the too-long legs of my overalls. The dead birds, hundreds and hundreds of them, were laid out on white paper or a white sheet. There were close-ups of some of them. I saw the back-turned legs and the way their beaks were half-open in a sort of death shriek. They could have been stuffed, lying there, but they were too ugly. I imagined somebody collecting them, maybe in a wheelbarrow, tipping them out, arranging them for the pictures. Gross! And yet somehow exciting too.

Winter Claghorn tipped his chair back. "It's expensive. But we got to figure how much the damn birds are costing us every day right now. We've reckoned it up and with the Bradleys and the Petersons and you and us it'll come to about four hundred apiece."

"The Jensens'll chip in, too, I'm pretty sure," Joe Dobbs said.

"When can you do it?" Dad asked Flit.

"Tomorrow, in the afternoon. I have the Avatril, and my plane's over at Benton. Joe here picked me up." He began gathering the pictures together. "Them dang birds is everywhere." He slid the glossy photographs back in the folder and his smile slanting down on me was quick and friendly. I couldn't think of him as a killer. "Good pictures, huh, boy?"

34

I nodded. "Real good."

"I'll draw up the contract and drop it off in the morning," Flit Crockett said. "And I'll pick up the money when the job's done."

Joe Dobbs stood up and punched my arm. "I hear you did some pretty fair shooting yourself this morning, Marcus. You're a chip off the old block."

"Yes, sir." The words came out good. I guess Joe Jr. had told him. I smiled my own killer smile.

"Bragging again, huh?" Dad said, and shook his head. There was a good, warm, friendly man-feeling in the kitchen now that Mom had gone. We could all hate the birds together.

Dad and I walked the men across the front yard to the road where Joe Dobbs's car was parked, and we didn't talk at all on the way back to the house.

The harsh jangle of the blackbirds' voices hung between us. When the birds had first come, before we'd known the heartache they'd bring with them, Mom had sung a sweet, sad little song. It had been the very first night, when we'd thought they were just making a stop and would be gone in the morning, and the sound of them was new and exciting and strange.

"Blackbird singing in the dark of night," Mom sang. I couldn't remember any of the rest of it except that it was something about taking us with it and teaching us to fly. But the sound they made wasn't singing. And who'd want to go with them?

There was a light in an upstairs window and Dad stared up at it.

"You know, I never minded a few birds around," he said. He seemed to be pleading with someone, and I knew it wasn't me. "But I can't just stand back and let a million of them eat our corn."

"Don't worry about it, Dad," I said. He didn't have to apologize to anyone. "Those damn birds are taking ten percent of our yield per acre."

Each word came out sharp and clear as a rifle shot. Heck, I was talking so good again I could have been a TV announcer.

5

I lay that night thinking about things. And as usual, when I was alone, I could see both sides of the question. Being able to see both sides at once was my biggest problem.

I listened to the birds, and I thought, poor Mom! And I knew how hard tomorrow was going to be for her. I thought about her bird painting, the dazzled look on her face as she sat in front of her easel watching the flock come back at sunset, and I knew that now the painting would never be finished. Poor Mom! It took me a long time to get to sleep, and it was the ringing of the alarm that pulled me awake again and away from the dream. Could it be morning? In my dream Mom had put a pie on the kitchen table, all crusty and steaming hot from the oven. Dad was sniffing at it. "Blackberry?" he asked.

"Huh-uh." Mom shook her head and she cut into the crust and blackbirds began flying out, silent blackbirds that glided like big, dark moths on motionless wings. They filled our kitchen, clinging to the tops of pictures, drifting above the table as though hanging from invisible strings.

"Four and twenty blackbirds baked in a pie," Mom said, and Dad hugged her in the old way and smiled down at her. "That's a terrific idea. We can eat them. Why didn't I think of that before?"

Mom put a slice in front of me and in the dream I was happy because all three of us were working together to get rid of the blackbirds. But the good feeling I'd had in the dream didn't stay when I wakened. I shivered. Blackbird pie!

My room was filled with the sad light of morning. In the trees outside the birds rustled and squawked, and for a minute I couldn't think why I'd wanted to be awake this early. Then I remembered. This was the last day, the very last day, and I would be looking at the morning birds for the last time.

I got out of bed and knelt by the window with my nose pressed against the glass.

The sky had a line across it. Above the line it gleamed, pale as a pearl, and the trees were etchings scored on a milky mirror. Below the paleness the dark hung, holding onto the night, and the line was like the horizon, the place that divided the land from the sky.

The birds were restless. Morning was calling and already a few of them circled, gliding between the dark and the day, crossing and recrossing the line. Did they know the line was there? Was it like moving from the night outside into a lighted room, and did the change come at that very second of flight? The birds were so splendid, so calm and beautiful, that they made my breath catch in my throat. I loved the birds. Soon now they would be gone.

My camera lay on top of my dresser. I took it and set the light meter and I opened the window that was never opened because of the smells, and I leaned my elbows on the sill to steady the shake in my hands. If the picture came out I'd be able to look at it after, and remember.

I was shivering and my throat hurt. I got quickly back into bed.

When I wakened the next time it was much later. I could tell by the way the sun slanted across the poster of Grandma. It was over the ankle straps of her shoes already, which meant it was after seven. An empty silence would be hard to get used to again.

I didn't feel good.

I lay still, counting myself off from top to bottom to find the trouble.

Well, my head knew that the birds would be poisoned today. Twenty thousand of them. They would lie between the green cornstalks and the little breeze that came in the evening would ruffle their dead feathers, and flies would suck from their glazed, jelly eyes. Flit Crockett would circle above in his plane and he'd be screaming down, "Know what I mean? Know what

I mean?" And that would be good, wouldn't it? The birds had to go. But we wouldn't lay them out on sheets and take pictures of them—dead. We wouldn't do that.

I let my thoughts jump down to my eyes. What if I got the blinks again? Last time the blinks had come with the stuttering. I could feel my eyes twitch. To think about the blinks was to have them. It was like floating on your back in the river and thinking about sinking. Right away you sank. But I had only had the stutters for a minute or two yesterday. Then they'd gone away. I wet my lips and said aloud, "Sam and Sabrina." Perfect. Then I said, "Poison the birds." Perfect again.

I swallowed. Yes, my throat hurt. And I had a memory of coughing in the night. I'd better not tell Mom how long I'd stayed in the river yesterday.

When I sniffed I could smell French toast, or maybe pancakes so I got dressed quickly and went downstairs. I hoped it was French toast.

Mom and Dad were in the kitchen and I heard them fighting. My feet slowed and the French toast didn't seem so great any more.

"Of course you didn't notice," Mom was saying. The door was a little open and I could hear every word. I wished they'd at least shut the door when they were fighting. "You don't notice anything any more. Not me. Not Marcus. Not anything but the birds. You are obsessed by those birds."

I stood on the bottom step listening to them and to

the sound of my heart beating. Once before I'd listened, hiding under the table where the red fringe hung. The memory of that made my heart beat faster now.

"*I'm* obsessed by the birds." Dad laughed a short, bitter laugh. "You're the one who's obsessed. Anyway, we're not talking about the birds, we're talking about Marcus."

"The stuttering's back," Mom said.

There was a stretch of waiting silence. I perched on the step like a blackbird on a stump. "He knows it's back. But he doesn't want us to know."

It isn't back, I wanted to shout. Sam and Sabrina. Poison the birds. Sister Susie's shelling eggs! A tickle feathered my throat and I needed badly to cough.

"Maybe . . . maybe you should take him in again to see Kelsey," Dad said.

Oh no, not Kelsey. I didn't want to see Kelsey.

"And maybe we should just give up," Mom said. "We should stop putting him through things like this."

What did they mean, give up? Give up, give up, give up?

My cough came so suddenly and so sneakily that I had no time to gather it back. Its force scattered the germs that danced in the light from the hall window, turning them over and over, leaving a clean, unpolluted passage for me to walk through.

Dad pushed the kitchen door farther open. "Morning, Marcus."

"Morning, Dad." I went past him trying to look as if

41

I'd just come down the stairs and hadn't been standing there listening.

Give up, give up, give up? What did they mean, give up?

I sat down in my usual chair at the table and then I remembered that this was where Flit Crockett had sat last night. I shifted seats. What was the matter with me? Last night I'd liked him. Last night I'd thought what he did was pretty neat.

"You look flushed." Mom put a hand on my forehead. "You were coughing in the night."

"I was?" I asked.

"It might be a good idea to drive in and let Kelsey have a look at you," Mom said, and I was mad because she was trying to make it seem as if she'd just thought of that, and that she wanted me to see Kelsey because of the cough and not for anything else.

"I d-d-d-don't want to s-s-see K-K-Kelsey!"

I looked up at her and I felt the tears coming and then I thought I felt the blinks. I'd forgotten how awful the blinks were, but I remembered again real fast. My eyes would begin to flicker and the kitchen would flutter around me. I raised my eyebrows and put all my force into making my eyeballs stay still, but I knew if they didn't want to they wouldn't. "It's your autonomic nervous system," Kelsey had said, which meant I had no control over it. Like hiccups. I leaned my elbows on the table and stretched my eyes apart, with my thumbs pulling down on the lower lids and my fingers lifting up on the top ones, just in case it was starting.

Mom cradled my head against her front and I wriggled, trying to get inside her, into the softness and the blackness.

The blinks still hadn't come when I pulled away. Mom held on to my hands. Her mouth was squashy. "Kelsey helped before. She could give you some more of those pills."

"He'll be all right when the birds go," Dad said, and that was Dad and me on the same thought wave again. "The birds are what's driving us all crazy."

Mom blazed up at him. "Oh, how can you be so stupid, Sam? Kill the birds. Poison them. Blow them to pieces. It's all the birds' fault. Can't you see the birds are just a whipping boy for us . . . for what's wrong?"

She stopped, and I wished she'd let go of my hands so they'd be ready in case of the blinks. I could feel them coming. My eyelids were moving gently, like butterflies wakening.

"It *is* the b-birds," I said, and I hated Mom. Why couldn't she see that? Why couldn't she understand that when they went everything would be O.K. again?

Dad was leaning over the table. A vein stretched blue along the side of his neck. "You hear that cough of Marcus's? You ever think what that might be? Just a summer cold, huh? Ever think it might be histoplasmosis?

43

Bird disease, from the droppings your beautiful birds are leaving around our house? Disease, Sabrina! Spores, growing in that filth!"

They stared at each other. Mom's face was tight and white. This was the worst one yet, the worst, the very worst.

"Don't do this to us, Sam. Marcus just has a cold."

"I s-s-stayed too l-l-long in the r-r-river," I stuttered. "Wh-what's histo—histo?"

Dad stepped back. He ran his hand across his face and smoothed away the vein. "Better have Kelsey take some x-rays anyway." His voice was tired. "I'm sorry, Marcus. I'm sure you just have a cold." He was staring at me as if he didn't see me. "It used to be when we got you between us it was to love you and keep you safe. Now . . . well, now I don't know what it's for." He straightened up. "I'll take care of your chores today, Marcus, along with my own. Sabrina, you can take the truck and go into town."

Mom stood looking down at the table when he left. I couldn't see what she was looking at.

What if they did give up? What would happen to me? Suddenly I began to cough and it was as if I'd never stop.

Mom got me a glass of orange juice.

Then she went to the phone and I listened to her arrange for Kelsey to see me at eleven.

"Oh, he's got a cold and a fever," she said. "And other things."

Why don't you tell her, Mom? Stutters and histo-whatever and maybe blinks on the way.

I imagined Kelsey tapping her pencil on her desk, the sun gleaming on her glasses, her white coat with the creases in it sharp as the ones in Flit Crockett's slacks.

"I'm too b-b-big now for a lady d-d-doctor," I said. "What if she m-makes me t-take off my p-pants?"

"She won't. And you know she's just about the best doctor there is, Marcus. And she's our friend. She cares about us."

She fixed me fresh French toast but I couldn't eat it because of how much my throat hurt. Kelsey cared about us all right. About one of us.

Later, after I'd had my shower and dressed all over again in clean underwear and a clean T-shirt, I tried to look up histo in my Oxford Dictionary that Mom had bought for me at Mr. Townsberry's auction. But I didn't know how to spell it. I did find "whipping boy." It said, "One who was reared with a young prince and beaten in his stead when he committed a fault that deserved flogging."

I tried to figure it out. If the birds were the whipping boy, who was the prince?

6

Joe Jr.'s mom called just as we were ready to go and I heard Mom tell her that sure, we'd pick up some cough medicine for Joe Jr. at Ballantine's Drugs. Since we were stopping at the drugstore I ran back upstairs to get my film. It was weird that Joe Jr. had a cough too. Maybe we both had histo.

The phone call made us late and we didn't even take time to lift the bales of hay from the back of the truck before we took off. Mom said we mustn't keep Kelsey waiting. It wouldn't be fair since she was seeing us on such short notice.

Kelsey! I was sweating, just thinking about talking to her. As soon as she heard my stutters she'd know Mom and Dad were doing badly again. And I sure hoped she'd say that all I had was a cold.

I sat in the truck next to Mom, sucking on a piece of ice. Mom had filled a wide-necked thermos with cubes so I'd have them for the trip. My mouth and tongue felt numb, but the ice really helped my throat.

Mom was wearing lipstick, which made her look different. I wanted to ask her if we'd be home in time for the poisoning. She'd think me horrible for wanting to be there. She'd think I was a monster. Maybe I was. But I'd probably never again have the chance to see a plane spraying our cornfields, and twenty thousand birds falling dead from the skies.

I could smell the good, spicy tomato and vinegar smell that drifted from the Pure 'n' Fresh canning plant. Elderberries hung in dusty purple clusters on the fence rows and blackbirds flared above the tall green stalks of our corn. From this far away they looked motionless, like the ones that had flown out of our blackbird pie.

"There used to be hawks," Mom said softly. "The hawks scared away the blackbirds. But we used pesticides to get rid of the hawks. I suppose, in the spring, when there are no blackbirds to keep down the insects we'll use insecticides to get rid of the bugs that eat our seed."

Course she was exaggerating. Twenty thousand dead blackbirds didn't mean there'd be none left. I tried to figure what eighty percent of a million would be, left flying around, but I couldn't handle it. And that would be only ours. Multiply that a jillion times.

"T-t-there's a b-b-blackbird explosion," I said.

We were stopped at a stop sign. "Every living thing in the world is a part of the great mystery of creation," she said. "When will humans recognize that?" She

ground the gears when we were taking off again and I heard the bales of hay in the back slide and slither. "There's a people explosion, too, you know," she said. "Maybe we could hire that . . . that . . ." Her throat moved as she swallowed. "He could spray the cities. Only two percent though. That'll be enough for now."

I stared out of the window. We were going through Poppy Point. I'd come to a rodeo here once with Dad and the Dobbses and a bunch of other people. Mom had been the only mother missing. She said rodeos were cruel. Dad told everyone she had a headache, but I bet they all knew. They probably all thought she was weird.

"You should never have married her," Kelsey had said that one time, that one awful time. "She's not right for you, Sam. We're right for each other. Us, Sam. You and me."

It was on New Year's Eve, last New Year's, and I was under the table. Mom had made her New Year's champagne punch. I'd had a glass of it along with everybody else as the clock struck midnight. The glass bowl had been left on the dining room table and all night people had been drifting in and out helping themselves. I'd been helping myself, too, ducking under the table with my plastic cup to drink in secret. I'd had two refills already and it was getting harder and harder to crawl under the table without spilling the punch. I was feeling terrific but sort of strange in an O.K. way. There's something real nice about being somewhere you're not supposed to be when everyone thinks you're somewhere else, like in bed, and doing something you're not supposed to be doing, like drinking, and being all private and secret and watching the world go by. I was leaning against the round pedestal of the table thinking about how impressed Joe Jr. would be when I told him I got sloshed at New Year's when I saw two more pairs of feet coming through the door. A man's feet and a woman's feet. The brown Hush Puppy shoes were Dad's, but the red high heels weren't anything Mom would have. They didn't come over to the table. They stopped, brown toes almost touching red toes.

That was when I heard Kelsey's voice, the excitement in it, the urgency. "Us, Sam. You and me."

I set down my cup and suddenly I didn't feel contented or pleased with myself any more. I wasn't drunk any more either. I guess I never had been. I'd been acting big, that was all.

The tablecloth was red with tassels on the edges. Mom had bought it for Christmas. I peered out, parting the tassels carefully with my fingers.

Dad and Kelsey stood under the piece of withered mistletoe. They were wearing the paper hats that Mom had given out at midnight.

Kelsey's arms were twined around Dad's neck.

I saw the watch on her wrist. It was the one she checked when she counted my pulse. Her lips were moving.

Dad's back was to me, but they were standing sort of

sideways so Kelsey wasn't hidden. Her hat was a black pirate's one and her short blonde hair curled around the sides of it. I couldn't see her eyes because her glasses were misted.

Dad's hat was tall and green. I'd laughed when he put it on. He looked like the Jolly Green Giant. But Kelsey wasn't laughing.

"Sam! Sabrina doesn't belong in your life here."

Why wasn't Dad pulling away from her? Why didn't he bop her one for saying that about Mom? All right for Dad to say it, stroking Mom's face, smiling down at her. But not Kelsey, Kelsey wasn't even a part of our family.

Why didn't he tell her what a good farmer's wife Mom was in a bunch of ways? How she'd disked close to a hundred acres in our big John Deere 4020 this spring? How she'd helped make hay? The way she worked in her bean patch till her hands bled and she could hardly straighten up? So what if she was different from a lot of other women around here? When we walked the fields together she talked to me about the cycles of life. About the plowing and the planting and the harvesting. About the wonder of putting a little seed in the ground and having it come up and be a bright red tomato or an orange marigold with a black center. She loved the farm as much as we did. Why didn't he tell rotten old Kelsey that? It was because they'd had the gigantic row about the tree before

Christmas, Mom and Dad, and things were really, really bad. Mom had wanted to cancel the New Year's party, but Dad said no, they'd planned it and it had to go on. Maybe he'd just wanted to see Kelsey, to stand under the mistletoe with her.

I let the tassels close a little more in case they saw me.

"She's a child, Sam. A lovely, lovely child," Kelsey said. "You need a woman. Someone who understands you. And she's not good for Marcus either. She's destroying the boy."

Dad, Dad! Don't let her say it.

"But I love her, Kelsey," Dad said, and I pulled all the way back into my red under-table cave. I hugged my arms tight around myself and pretended I was happy. See? Dad loves Mom. He doesn't want you putting your arms around him. One in the snoot for you, kissy Kelsey! But something was wrong and I tried not to think about it. I couldn't help it. It was the way Dad had said the words. They hadn't come out all joyful, in a whoop and a holler. He'd said them the way I'd say, "Christmas is over" or "School starts tomorrow." Nothing happy there. Just something that couldn't be helped, couldn't be changed.

I wanted to peek out again and see if Kelsey had taken her arms away, but I was afraid. It was awfully quiet out there. What if they were kissing, one of those long, TV kisses with their eyes closed and their mouths open?

Hateful Kelsey, pretending to be Mom's friend, always talking to Mom about things that had happened when they'd been in school together. I couldn't stand her. And today she was going to be poking at me, asking me questions, looking at me with her sneaky little eyes.

Mom pulled the truck to the side of the road and stopped. We had arrived.

Hamden Medical Clinic, the sign read. A small white card stuck on the door announced, "Closed September 4 for Labor Day." I wished it was Labor Day now so we could go home. There was a black panel at the side where all the doctors' names were listed, with what they did printed next to them.

Kelsey was just a plain old doctor. Kelsey Lee, M.D. She was nothing special at all. Just because she'd been smart in school didn't mean she hadn't slowed down since.

Mom told the receptionist that we had an appointment and she took us down a corridor filled with doors to Kelsey's office. There were the usual, clean, sick-making smells, like the Monday-morning bathrooms in school.

Kelsey rose from behind her desk and held out her hands to Mom. They kissed each other's cheeks, open-eyed, closed-mouthed. I was practicing saying "Hello, Kelsey" under my breath. If I didn't stutter over that *K* I might be able to fool her. Especially if I didn't talk much, and I sure didn't want to talk much to her anyway. But of course I did stutter. It was just about the worst stutter yet. I sounded like a train picking up speed on its way out of the station.

Kelsey smiled. It was supposed to show me she was friendly and sympathetic, but I knew different.

"You know, Marcus, after your mom called, I decided it would be better if you saw Dr. Green instead of me. He has just joined our staff and he . . . specializes in cases like yours."

"C-c-colds?" I asked. "Or the histo st-stuff?"

"No," Kelsey said. "That's not what I meant." She turned to Mom. "I guessed his stuttering was back, Sabrina. I could give him more tranquilizers, but it would be better to get to the root of the trouble."

I'd remember to look on the name board on the way out to see what kind of a doctor Dr. Green was. Something fancier than Kelsey. And what did she mean "root of the trouble"? Mom and Dad were my roots. Kelsey better keep her hands off them. And Dr. Green better keep his off too.

"Histoplasmosis?" Kelsey said, and I knew I'd missed part of their conversation. "Is that what you're worried about?"

"Sam thinks Marcus might have it."

Kelsey laughed. In anybody else it would have been an O.K. laugh, kind of tinkly. In Kelsey it sounded to me like someone ripping aluminum foil.

"Oh, that Sam!" she said.

I wanted to leap on her and break her dumb glasses. Didn't Mom notice the mushy way she said Dad's name?

I swallowed and discovered that my throat was hurting more.

Kelsey shook down a thermometer and put it in my mouth. "Are you and Sam still fighting over the birds?" she asked Mom.

Don't tell her, I wanted to say. But I couldn't, and anyway the thermometer was in my mouth.

Mom nodded. Then Kelsey nodded, too, all understanding. "Sam's just trying to put a scare in you. Histoplasmosis is pretty rare. And usually the spores only spread after the birds have gone. They live in old droppings that have lain undisturbed for a long time." She took out the thermometer and put it in some pink stuff in a jar. "It has symptoms like flu and it's pretty nasty. But it responds well to antibiotics. We'll just listen to your chest, big guy," she said to me. "Got to please your old man." I hated people who said "we" instead of "I." Nobody was going to listen to my chest except her. And I hated ladies who used kid talk, like "old man" and "big guy." I hated Kelsey.

"Sit up on the table and peel off your shirt, Marcus."

I took it off and perched on her black table with the strip of white paper rolled along it. You could probably lay out fifty dead birds on that paper and get a pretty good picture. I sure hoped we'd be home in time.

Kelsey put the stethoscope plugs in her ears.

"The birds are going to be killed today," Mom told her mournfully, but Kelsey didn't hear because her ears were stuffed.

The stethoscope was cold on my chest and back.

What if Mom and Dad did give up? What if he married Kelsey? She'd be a mean stepmother all right. Our whole house would smell like the school bathroom. She'd probably think eggs were healthy and make me eat them. And she wouldn't mind things being killed around the farm. Doctors saw dead things all the time.

"There's a bit of congestion," Kelsey said, taking the stethoscope out of her ears and letting it dangle round her neck. "But it's nothing to worry about." She peered down my throat, and in my ears and up my nose.

"I think it's just a cold, Sabrina. But we'll get some x-rays and run a couple of tests since the birds *have* been around. We don't want to take any chances. While he's in with Jim Green, you and I can have a cup of coffee and talk."

The way she said "talk" was a dead giveaway. She wanted Mom to tell her everything. And Mom would. She trusted Kelsey. She thought she was her friend.

"D-d-don't talk to her, M-Mom," I said. "D-d-don't tell her anything."

"Marcus!" Mom's face was red.

Kelsey was staring at me with a strange, questioning

look and I stared right back at her, holding my shirt in front of me for protection. I know about you, I told her silently, and then I saw her face begin to redden and I knew my message had reached her. She knew I knew how she felt about Dad.

"He's . . . not himself, Kelsey," Mom said. She pushed back her hair. "None of us is."

Kelsey patted Mom's shoulder. "You come with me, Marcus," she said. "We'll have our x-rays taken and then I'll introduce you to Dr. Green."

I followed her along the corridor.

"X-rays don't hurt, Marcus," Kelsey said, handing me over to a skinny guy in a white coat. "It's just like having your picture taken."

"I know," I said. Just because I stuttered, did she think I was a dummy?

I stared at the closed door after she left. She was probably going back to persuade Mom to give up, to leave Dad, to move out so she could move in.

My throat hurt so bad I wished I'd brought the ice in with me from the truck.

7

After the x-rays and the blood tests Kelsey took me to Dr. Green's office. There was a little glass place outside where his nurse sat, and a waiting room inside. I stayed there while Kelsey went in through Dr. Green's private door.

In a few seconds she came back and said to me, "Dr. Green would like to talk to your mom first, Marcus. I'll go get her."

"Wh-what does he w-want to talk to her for?" I asked. "Sh-she doesn't st-stutter."

Kelsey smiled her rotten, understanding smile.

Mom came back with her, looking worried, and Kelsey knocked again and ushered Mom inside where I guessed Dr. Green crouched waiting, like a spider in his web.

"She won't be long," Kelsey said to me. "Can you find something to read?"

I nodded and picked up a *Boys' Life*. I turned the

pages, seeing nothing of the words or the pictures, my ears straining for some sound coming from behind the closed door. But there was nothing to hear and I figured it must be sound-proofed in case somebody screamed.

There was a hopeless, sinking feeling inside me. Dr. Green was probably advising Mom to give up too. There was no way I could fight them all, him and Kelsey and Mom herself. Oh, Mom! And it was my fault. If I didn't stutter and get the blinks then we wouldn't be here because nobody would know I cared about their fighting.

A little kid about seven came in the waiting room with his mom. His name was Billy. I found out pretty soon because his mom was all the time saying, "Don't do this, Billy. Don't do that."

"What's your name?" he asked me.

"M-M-Marcus."

"Do you wet the bed too?"

I held tightly to the magazine. "N-no," I said. "I just have a c-cough." I wished he'd go away and quit putting ideas in my head.

"I've got a Yo-Yo." He produced it from his pocket. When he looped the cord around his finger and let go the Yo-Yo bounced off the floor.

It made me laugh. "Here," I said. I took it and stood up, rewinding the string.

I was pretty good with a Yo-Yo. Joe Jr. and I had a craze for them a couple of years back and I used to be

able to do "Dead Man's Swing" and "Loop the Loop."
I was out of practice though.

"You're not too hot." Billy grabbed for it back.

He swung the Yo-Yo under my nose. "Watch this."

The string had knotted and he was getting mad at it.
He squatted at my feet, his skinny little fingers picking,
picking, making the knots worse. His nails were bitten down till there was no trace of them. It probably
went with the bed-wetting.

I just about jumped out of my chair when he flung
the Yo-Yo at the wall and began screaming. I don't
know where he'd learned the words. Even Hubie
Keller didn't know that many good words.

The nurse came hurrying from her little glass cage.
She got Billy a glass of water and produced a box of
graham crackers. I began coughing, so she brought me
some water too.

The Yo-Yo had bounced close to my feet. It really
bugged me, lying there in its mess of knotted string. I
picked it up.

Billy's mother eyed me coldly. "Just put it in the
wastebasket," she said. I saw her fear that I would get
Billy started again.

I coaxed at the knots with my nails and teeth. Too
bad I didn't have Joe Jr. here. With his teeth we'd
have had it made. But Joe Jr. was at home, probably
watching for Flit Crockett. I imagined the birds, flying low over our fields, stopping to drink from the

milky sweetness of our corn kernels. The birds, their wings skimming against the sunlight, flying in their own sun shadows, the big, black plane bearing down on them.

The inner door opened and Mom came out with a man. He was wearing a corn-colored corduroy jacket instead of a white coat, but I knew he was Dr. Green. Who else could he be? He had a black mustache and black curly hair and he was the littlest man I'd ever seen. He was littler than Mom. Littler than me. He'd make a great jockey if he knew how to ride. Nobody could be afraid of someone that little. But I was.

I stood up, clutching the Yo-Yo.

Mom had chewed off her lipstick and her face was pale.

"Marcus?" Dr. Green said, and I nodded.

"Come on in." Under the jacket he wore a red shirt and a red bow tie. Some weird doctor.

"Gimme back my Yo-Yo," Billy said.

"Here," I said. "It's almost unt-tangled. Don't give up on it, B-Billy."

I walked past Mom into Dr. Green's office and he closed the door behind me and leaned against it.

"Why was it so important to untangle the string, Marcus?" His head was cocked on one side, and all at once, standing there with his black hair and his red shirt, I knew he wasn't a spider at all. He was a black-bird. Today the blackbirds would be poisoned, twenty thousand of them!

"I d-d-don't know," I said. "I d-don't like to give up on th-things that can be s-saved."

"I see." Dr. Green waved me to a chair in front of a desk. "Let's talk, Marcus."

I sat in the chair. It was a big, slumpy one. I hoped Dr. Green never slouched in it or he'd disappear forever. He perched on the edge of his desk, letting his legs dangle.

"How are things?" he asked.

"O-k-k-kay." I studied the right knee of my jeans, rubbing it in a circle with my finger. Why had I wasted all that time out in the waiting room? I should have been planning what to say so he'd leave my roots alone, so he'd think the stuttering grew from something else. I was always pretty good at knowing the right thing to say to get the best answer. Like in the Sunday papers, the part where there are quizzes so you could find out about yourself. You could make them come out any way you liked. On the one to see how long you'd live— I made it come out so I'd live to a hundred and eighty-three. And on the one to test how you were as a lover, I was "super stud," and I hardly even talk to girls yet. But this test was for real. I thought I felt the blinks coming. I wished I'd taken time to go to the bathroom instead of playing with that dumb Yo-Yo. I needed to go so bad now it hurt.

"Do you like baseball?" Dr. Green asked.

I stared at the question, turning it round and round before I answered. I couldn't find any tricks in it.

"P-p-pretty much," I said.

He nodded and smiled as if I'd really pleased him.

"What else do you like?"

I'd soon have a nice hole poked in the knee of my jeans. I bored at it, keeping my head down, pretending my finger was a screwdriver. "S-s-swimming."

"Swimming's great," he said. "Especially where there's a river. We had a river where I lived when I was a boy. Do you ride inner tubes?"

I nodded again and let myself sink a little farther into the chair. I was doing O.K. The thing was to give one-word answers, two at the most.

We talked about mini-bikes and the Indians' chances for the pennant and school. At least *he* talked. I did my one-word bit.

He wasn't a bad guy. A lot better than Kelsey. I wondered if he did ordinary doctor things as well as problem stuff. I'd sure as heck rather have him looking up my nose than Kelsey.

Then he said, kind of offhand, "Your mother tells me you're a good artist."

I began poking at my other knee. There was a trap here. Had she told him I was just like her? I swallowed, and the prickle in my throat stung and made me cough. Did she remember to tell him that I was a good shot, too, like Dad? It was no fair having her in without him. And it was no fair to me not knowing what she'd said. Did she tell Dr. Green about the way I'd killed

64

the blackbird, its head flying off, the rest of it falling in a sticky glued mess of feathers?

"I can d-d-draw o-k-k-kay," I said.

Dr. Green walked around his desk and came back with a big pad of drawing paper and a charcoal pencil. He waited politely while I finished coughing, then set the pad and pencil on my knees.

"Nasty cough," he said. "Did Dr. Lee give you something for it?"

"We're g-g-getting something from the d-drugstore."

"Do me a favor, Marcus. Draw your family for me. Just draw them the way you see them, the way you feel about them. The reason I'm asking you to do this is because it's sometimes easier to draw what we feel than to put it into words." He smiled. "And I don't mean because of the stutter. I mean because some things live way deep inside of us. And sometimes, too, in talking there are all kinds of stumbling blocks." His sleek black eyebrows lifted. "You know, even love can be a stumbling block."

He walked to the other side of the desk. "I'll leave you alone while I make a phone call." I picked up the pencil before it could roll off and I stared at the blank, cream-colored paper. It was like looking at a smooth, innocent stretch of quicksand. One wrong step here and I'd be sucked under.

Dr. Green sat in a tan-colored desk chair. He had dialed the phone and swiveled the chair around so his back was to me, but that didn't fool me a bit. Paying no attention? Like heck! That's what he wanted me to think. He probably had a secret mirror. And for a while there I was beginning to think he was O.K. I concentrated on hiding my panic and I said to myself, as if I were reading, "Do you favor one parent over the other? Which way is it in your family? Draw us a picture and we'll tell you." But it's probably easier to fool the dumbos on the Sunday paper than to fool Dr. Green.

I carefully drew Mom, her long straight black hair, her pretty face. I wasn't able to make it as pretty as it really is, of course. I'm not *that* good. I had her smiling a big, wide smile and looking out of the page. It was a smile I hadn't seen in a long time, but Dr. Green wouldn't know that. Nothing there that he could find anything wrong with.

Then I drew Dad beside her, the same size and everything. I had him smiling, too, and I had his arm around Mom's shoulder. "See," he seemed to say, "see how happy we are?" I sat back to admire it and then I remembered. I was supposed to be in the picture too. I'd used up almost all the room. There was a tiny margin on either side. If I put me next to Mom that would probably mean something. If I put me next to Dad that would probably mean something else. I could imagine the Sunday paper explaining it all in that smug way of theirs.

I closed my eyes and chewed on the pencil. Help! Help! From somewhere I seemed to hear Mom's voice saying, "Maybe we should just give up. We should stop putting him through things like this." No, Mom, it's O.K. Honest!

"Great," Dr. Green said into the phone. The swivel chair moved a little as if he was impatient to say goodby and hang up. "That'll be fine," he said.

I quickly penciled me in between the two of them. It was a bit squashed, but better than not being there at all, which would probably mean I was nothing. I put the pencil down.

"Finished?" Dr. Green asked.

He set the phone on the hook and walked around the desk, and already I wished I had done something better.

Too late! Like always when you handed in a test paper.

Dr. Green picked up the pad and tilted his little blackbird head to look at the picture.

"Good of your mom," he said. "She wasn't kidding, you are an artist. Can't say about your dad 'cause I haven't met him yet."

Yet!

I knew he'd come to *me*.

And his eyes were soft as could be. I wondered how come.

His head tilted even more. "Strange the way you drew your legs." He turned the picture toward me and I saw I'd made my legs all bendy, like a cowboy who'd sat too long on a horse. Why had I done that? I looked at it again and suddenly I knew. I knew how I saw myself.

I opened my mouth and closed it again. Dr. Green was probably better at puzzles than anybody. Figuring them was his job. I had a horrible, sure feeling that it wouldn't take him long at all to figure out this one.

8

We didn't talk much on the way home, Mom and I, except that Mom asked, "How did you like Dr. Green?" and I said, "He s-seems O.K."

"He wants to see us again," she said. "All of us. Dad too."

"I know." I looked out the window. Dr. Green and Kelsey, digging away at us. I imagined Dr. Green taking out my drawing, looking at it, clapping his hands to his head and shouting, "I've got it. I know what that boy is. They have to let go or he'll be destroyed." He'd phone up and say, "Mr. and Mrs. Miles, I want you to give up. You must separate for Marcus's sake. He'll stutter and stammer and blink forever if you don't. He may even begin bed-wetting, or worse."

"Which one of us should have him?" Mom talking with her mouth all squashy.

"Well, I see from the picture that he drew for me that he favors both of you equally. But I've talked it over with Dr. Lee who is such a good friend of your family, and she says he'd be better with his dad. She'll be happy to keep an eye on them."

Mom was pulling the truck into the Dobbs's yard, and for the first time in a long while I remembered about the birds.

"Wh-what t-time is it?" I asked.

"Ten after two."

No one seemed to be home, so she left Joe Jr.'s bottle of Winston Cough Syrup on top of Mrs. Dobbs's washer.

I ran up to Joe Jr.'s bedroom just in case, but it was empty, so I knew his cold and cough weren't that bad that he'd had to stay home and miss the poisoning. I bet his parents hadn't made *him* get x-rays.

I took the stairs back down two at a time. "L-let's h-hurry," I told Mom. I stared up at the sky but there was no plane in sight, only the clear, hot, blue emptiness of summer. What if it was all over?

We drove out of the Dobbses' yard slow as sludge. I looked sideways at Mom, letting my anger build. She'd be glad if I missed it. She was going slow on purpose.

"C-can't you d-drive f-faster?" I muttered.

Mom's lips tightened. We drove through the tomato and vinegar smell, and there was our big silo and our fields. I saw Dad standing over to the side in a cluster of people.

Mom had seen him, too, but she wasn't stopping.

"L-let me out," I said.

"Don't you want to come home and eat something? You must be starved."

"N-n-no."

Mom drew the truck to the side of the road and I was out almost before she stopped. Dad waved, and I heard the truck roar away behind me. The gray of its exhaust hung smelly in the heat, but over the engine's roar I heard something else—the low, faraway drone of a plane.

I stood where I was by the roadside. Black-eyed Susans, tall as my knees, drooped their heavy heads. A few purple gentians straggled through the long grass. In the cornfield beyond the fence, blackbirds fluttered up in groups of ten or twenty, calling to one another, settling again.

A small, silver plane no bigger than a bug hummed across the emptiness of the sky.

Dad waved and yelled, "Come on, Marcus. Here he is."

But I stood where I was, gripping the top strand of fence wire, feeling it hot and cutting against my hands.

The plane came low over our field.

Its noise disturbed the birds and they rose, squawking their anger, then dropped again. There were a lot of birds in our field today, probably a couple of thousand, waiting to die.

The plane circled, then came back, and this time it

spread a tail of poisoned corn chop in a wide sweep behind it. The kernels dropped thickly, like a hail of golden ice.

The birds rose together at the plane's coming, screaming, banking first to the left, then to the right in a noisy, fluttering shrill of blackness, a moving cloud that parted and separated and scattered to straggle back into our ripening corn.

The plane turned and made another sweep, and another, dropping its deadly cloud behind it in a pattern, straight as the furrows left by a plough. So many barrels per square foot, I'd heard Flit Crockett tell Joe Jr.'s dad, the deaths all worked out with pencil and paper. The birds flew up and flew down, veering from each new path that the plane took.

But now they could eat undisturbed. The design was finished. It had only taken about five minutes.

I watched the plane glide away, growing smaller with the distance, and I figured it was going toward Claghorn's, so they must be next. Look out, blackbirds, Flit Crockett's coming. Better fly now while you've got the chance.

Our field slept quietly again, sun-mellowed, beautiful. A few blackbirds drifted lazily above the corn, sailing down to hide themselves in its fresh greenness. It was as it had always been.

I let go of the fence wire. Its mark lay red across my palms, ridged into them.

"Hey, Marcus," Dad called.

I walked slowly to where they stood.

"Did you see it?" he asked.

I nodded.

"Well, I guess we'll just wait around and find out what happens next." Then it was as if he suddenly remembered.

"What did Kelsey say?"

I couldn't look at him any time he said Kelsey's name. "Sh-she th-thinks it's just a c-cold."

"Sure. That's all it is. I shouldn't . . ." He stopped. "Did she take x-rays?"

"And a b-bunch of t-tests. Mom b-bought me some Winston C-cough S-s-syrup."

"Good." I wanted to tell him about Dr. Green, to warn him, to catch hold of his arm and say, "Don't listen to him or to Kelsey or to anyone. Just listen to me. I'll be worse if you and Mom give up. I'll get things wrong with me you've never even heard of." But I didn't.

Dad lowered his voice and half turned from the others. "Is your mom O.K.? Is she very upset . . . about the birds?"

"I g-guess so." Now my anger was hot against *him.* What did he expect me to say? He knew she was upset over the birds. Did he think something magical had happened to change her? Mom would never change.

"You just got here in time, boy," Mr. Ebenhauser

said. His farm was about twelve miles from ours. I didn't know if he was in on the blackbird killing or not. Probably not, because if Flit Crockett had been spraying his fields today he'd have been there watching instead of here. His two daughters, Karen and Patty, stood on the other side of him. They were older than me, but I'd be starting their school in the fall.

"Hi," they said, like a chorus.

"H-hi." I looked at the faces and I knew everybody here. Course most people around here knew everybody else. There weren't that many farms.

"How long do you think it'll be before the birds begin to die?" Karen asked me.

I shrugged. When I had the stutters I used more shrugs and nods and head shakes than most people used in their whole lives.

We all stood around, waiting and sweating. The only sound was the sound of my coughing. Mr. Ebenhauser had a big, black circle under each armpit.

I took off my shirt and tied the sleeves around my waist, and I looked at the red-blue mark on the inside of my elbow where the blood had been sucked out through the needle this morning in the testing, and I thought, what if the Avatril doesn't work this time? What if everything stays the same, and we stand here and stand here and nothing happens? What if tonight the birds come winging back at sunset, darkening the sky, crowding themselves, black and shining, into our trees? A great well of joy seemed to rise inside me and spill over. I didn't want the birds to die, to lie stiff and rigid, their legs turned backward. But a horrible something thrust itself up through the joy, a niggle of disappointment. There'd be nothing to see then. No dead birds. No excitement.

"Look!" Karen pointed.

A blackbird rose into the sky, climbing straight and stiff, like a model plane. It towered up there and began to scream, the screams high-pitched and shrill with fear.

Something curdled, slowly and sickeningly, in my stomach.

The bird was shirring and whirring now, a toy windmill blurring in its own breeze, and all the time it shrieked those terrible, aching shrieks.

I saw another one rise, and it, too, climbed past the sky's blueness to where the heat haze hung, and when its screaming began I put my hands tight against my ears.

The rest of the flock, the ones that weren't in that doomed two percent, rose a few feet above the corn, floated there, their wings beating slowly, their heads cocked, uttering their own cautious warning cries to each other.

Now a third crazed bird was up, lofting above the field and the jabbering flock, zigzagging and somersaulting and adding its wild maddened cries to the cries of the other two. And a fourth now, and a fifth, and there were two layers of birds, the doomed ones above, the denser cloud below. The top layer was a nightmare of motion, and they weren't birds, they were only a whirling, writhing haze of pain.

I shaded my eyes with my hand, and I tried to look away, to look at something else, but the faces around me were almost worse than the nightmare above. There were open mouths, and staring eyes, and an excitement. In some of them there was almost a pleasure.

I wanted to go home.

"Isn't this something?" Mr. Ebenhauser kept muttering. "Never saw anything like this in all of my life. Isn't this something?"

I missed the first bird fall. It made no sound when it

hit the ground, and the thick cornstalks opened and closed over it as if to deny its death. I saw the others fall, dropping dark from the summer skies.

And I saw the flock go.

They stayed together, darting back and forth in black waves, undecided. One led. Then it was as if the vote had been taken, and the flight screamed away across our barn, and our yard, and the fields where our two cows grazed. The cows would be glad to see them go. The hogs too. The birds ate the slop from their feeding trough. Everyone would be glad to see the birds go. Except. . . .

I imagined Mom sitting by the kitchen table, hearing the rush of wings as the flight sailed across our house. She'd put her head on the table and her dark hair would spill across the dark wood. It's O.K., Mom. It's better this way. Things will be all right now, you'll see. But don't come down here and look at the dead ones. I won't look at them either.

In the field someone started a cheer, but it fizzled away into silence.

Dad's voice was flat. "Well," he said. "I guess it worked all right."

"You think they'll come back, Mr. Miles?" Patty asked him.

"Flit Crockett said no. And he's been right about everything so far."

A couple of the men said they were going to go among the corn and find the dead birds. They'd be tangled in the corn probably, hanging by a wing tip, their dead eyes staring. Or in between the rows, hidden maybe, so you'd step on one before you saw it.

"D-do we h-h-have to do-do that, D-Dad?"

"No." Dad put a hand on my shoulder. "We'll just go home."

"You want a ride back?" Mr. Ebenhauser asked, and I guessed he'd driven Dad over. "We're going now anyway. We'll drop on by the Claghorn place and see what's happening there. Or do you figure Crockett did their fields first?"

78

"I don't know," Dad said. "Anyway, Marcus and I'll just walk."

Mr. Ebenhauser's voice drifted after us as we walked away. "Wasn't that something, girls? That sure was something."

Dad and I tramped along the gravel road and then single file on the surfaced one that led to our house.

A solitary bird flew overhead. It was a grackle, and I looked at it and felt my stomach slip. Suppose it began climbing and cartwheeling and fell splattering at our feet? But it only chirped a few anxious, lonely chirps and skimmed on by.

"Th-they went th-thataway," I said.

Dad looked at me over his shoulder. "They're gone, Marcus. Know what I mean? Know what I mean? Know what I mean?" We laughed together and for the first time all day I felt happy.

9

It was sunset. The cows were milked and fed, the hogs were slopped, the day's work was over. Mom and Dad and I were all listening, each trying not to let the others see that that was what we were doing. Would the birds come back?

Outside, the day gleamed to an end and there was only the calm, shining silence of the summer evening.

I watched Mom when she didn't know I was watching and I thought, it's going to be O.K. now. The thing they've been fighting over is gone.

Both Mom and Dad were trying to be nice to each other. I could understand Dad trying, because that's the way it always was when he got his own way and when he knew his way had hurt Mom. But Mom usually came out of things slowly, like a spider that's been poked at and has to have time to uncurl. So something was different tonight. They even talked to each other over supper.

See? I thought. I knew it would be all right when we got rid of the birds, and the thought of the dead ones lying between the corn was a pleasure to me. Damn, dirty, noisy birds! Hey, we might even go black-berrying again, later on, when the berries were ripe. We might even see another unicorn.

About eight o'clock Dad said, "How about sitting out on the porch for a while? It's a lovely night."

We hadn't used the front porch in the evenings since the birds came because it was way too noisy to sit outside while they were in the trees.

Mom said, "I'll bring some lemonade," and Dad and I went out to dust off the chairs that hadn't been used since springtime.

The smell was bad.

Dad wrinkled his nose and said in a low voice, "We'll have to do something about those droppings, Marcus. Tomorrow we'll start spading them under."

"Yuk," I said. The last time I'd gone under the trees and looked, the muck had been inches deep. It would be up over our ankles now. I wondered if last winter's rubber boots still fit me. Winter, and the cold that seemed to go on forever. Winter, and Christmas.

It was a Christmas tree that had set off the last big row between Mom and Dad.

We always had a tinsel tree because Mom said it wasn't right to cut down a living one and bring it in the house. She said Christmas was a celebration of birth. Christmas was what we had inside of us and didn't depend on things like slaughtered pine trees. I was used to the tinsel tree and I didn't mind. What was under it was what was important—the gift boxes, begging to be opened.

But last Christmas Dad had gone out to a tree farm and he'd cut down a fourteen-foot silvertip and hauled it home in the back of our truck.

"I just had a hankering for the good smell of a live tree," he said, smiling in the way he did when he knew Mom was going to be mad.

Mom was sitting writing Christmas cards at the table. I knew she'd gone all the way into Dayton to Carleen's Gift Shop specially to buy them. They were stamped on the back, "These cards and envelopes are made entirely from reclaimed waste paper. No trees were destroyed to make them."

She'd looked up at the big pine Dad was dragging and her face had closed and she said, "Well, I hope you're happy then. You do know, though, that it's not alive any more."

Dad put the silvertip first in a bathtub of water and then in a round, wooden apple crate. He and I decorated it, and it did look terrific. Its smell filled our house, bringing the forest inside, and at night the firelight made shadows through it that lay like whispers across our kitchen walls and ceiling.

Mom touched the tree each time she passed it. "You

could have been a giant," she told it once. "You could have lived to be a hundred and two."

Dad felt bad and I did, too, because I enjoyed the tree so much.

Mom always knew the right thing to quote, and one night she stood under the silvertip and said dreamily, " 'The squirrel has leaped to another tree; the hawk has circled farther off, and has now settled upon a new eyrie, but the woodman is preparing [to] lay his axe to the root of that also.' "

Dad was drinking his after-supper coffee and he slammed his cup down so hard on the table it sloshed over. "You are totally irrational," he said. "We burn logs." His voice was tight with pushed-down anger. I wished he wouldn't be angry. Mom hadn't said that to hurt him. Beautiful words that she'd read stayed with her. It was just something that had lain in her head and that she'd remembered. "We only use firewood from trees that have already fallen," she said. "And if you can't see the difference between that and killing a tree to use as an ornament then there's nothing more to say."

"How about Happy Christmas?" Dad asked and slammed out.

I stood beside him now on the porch, and over to the side I could see the dark bulk of our compost heap. Somewhere under all of that lay the Christmas tree. I'd told Mom once that it was nice to think the silvertip would help now to grow other living plants and she'd hugged me and been pleased, and I was glad I'd thought of it, not only because she was comforted, but because it made me feel better too.

And Mom can have her maple trees back now, too, I thought. She'll be able to walk under them again, and watch their leaves change color, and their new growth come in the spring. That's another good thing about the birds going.

I sat down and tried not to breathe because the smells were really bad and for some reason they made my chest hurt more. I was glad when Dad said, "Maybe it wasn't such a good idea coming out here, Marcus. We're pushing things. It'll take a while for the stink to clear away."

I nodded and stood up in a fit of coughing.

"Have you taken any of your medicine?" Dad asked, but I couldn't answer because the cough was choking me. Through the screen door I saw Mom stirring the lemonade and pouring it into three glasses, and things seemed so much better, almost all right again.

She looked up when she heard me coughing, and she came on the porch.

"You sound terrible, Marcus? Does it hurt a lot?"

"N-n-not m-m-much," I lied.

She put her hand on my forehead. It was ice cold from the lemonade pitcher and it felt good, but her voice seemed to be coming from somewhere far away.

"I want you to go straight to bed," she said, and for once I didn't argue.

She brought me up honey tea with two big cloves floating in it.

Fred Johnson came to purr against my back, but for some reason I couldn't get to sleep. I kept thinking about the birds.

The quiet outside was suffocating me. I got out of bed and looked at the trees standing there, clumped against the paleness of the sky. They looked lonely.

In another place, far from here, the cloud of blackbirds had settled into other trees and other people would have watched them come, and there'd be that first excitement, that first breathtaking wonder at their beauty. I swallowed against the tightness in my throat.

10

The first thing I heard in the morning was the sound of men's voices downstairs. I got up and I was dizzy. I could smell my own breath each time I breathed. My pajamas were stuck to me and I wanted Mom.

She wasn't in the kitchen. I saw her outside with the basket, gathering eggs. Why was she doing that? That was my job.

Dad said, "Morning, Marcus," then went back to listening to the talk around the table.

Joe Dobbs was there and Winter Claghorn and Matt Jensen with his eldest boy, Henry.

"It just seems to me the only smart thing to do, Sam," Winter Claghorn said.

"I don't know what to say," Dad muttered. "Sabrina loves those trees."

I lifted my head, fearful of something, though I didn't know what.

"Flit says there's every chance the blackbirds will

come on this same flight pattern again next spring. And it's your trees they'll head for. None of the rest of us has a stand like that. We're all willing to share the costs with you. Fair's fair."

Henry Jensen grinned over at me. "See the fun yesterday, Marcus?"

I nodded. Yesterday and the bird-poisoning seemed so far away. There was a silver pin stuck in the arm of the chair. It had probably been there since Mom shortened my overalls—since she'd started to shorten my overalls. They never did get finished. I poked its point in and out of the chair arm. The little holes seemed to fuse together, then float apart.

"Wh-what do they w-want to d-do with the t-t-trees, D-Dad?" I asked.

"Cut 'em down." Dad ran his hands through his hair.

"Well, we don't want to have this damn poisoning to go through every year," Joe Dobbs said. "Though Flit was telling us another way of doing it so we could get rid of them in the spring and not have to sit around on our butts till they've eaten their way through our harvest. He says it works good in the cold weather. Do you remember the name of that poison, Winter?"

Winter shook his head. "I don't recall."

Their faces swam in front of me like a TV picture with bad reception.

"It does the job different," Joe Dobbs said. "Gets the birds in their roost. First Flit sprays them with this stuff, it's called Tergitol or something like that. It takes the oil out of their feathers. Then we spray the roost with water. Maybe even get the fire department to do it for us. The cold night temperature does the rest. The birds freeze to death right where they're roosting."

Matt Jensen chuckled. "We should have had some of that stuff before, when we were out there making fools of ourselves with the hoses."

"It wouldn't have done no good. You need the temperatures way down below freezing."

My fingers were slippery on the pin. What would Mom say? Oh, what would Mom say?

"With the trees down you and Joe Jr. could just about see each other's houses," Mr. Dobbs said to me.

I nodded, and my head almost fell off. I'd better not nod any more.

"It might be the best idea for you, Sam," Winter Claghorn added. "You could get the whole place ploughed under when they're through. The stink around here's something ferocious and that would make a good job of it."

"I'll talk it over with Sabrina," Dad said.

Dad would say to her, "It's the trees, Sabrina, the maples that you love. They have to be chopped down. It's that, or a million birds turned into living blocks of ice come spring."

It wasn't going to be all right, now that the birds were gone. Now there was something else. There always would be something else.

I saw all the days past and all the days ahead like

dead blackbirds, laid end to end on a roll of white paper.

There always would be something else.

I needed to go across to Dad, to stand next to him. I stood up, but my legs began to crimp underneath me, and then I said softly, "I'm a wishbone. Did you know that? By now Dr. Green knows. I drew him a picture. And you and Mom are pulling on me, pulling, and, well, the wishbone snapped. It just happened." I think I said it, but I'm not sure if I said the words out loud or not. I didn't hear them. But I did hear the thump I made when I smashed down on the kitchen floor.

I guess I have histoplasmosis. I guess Joe Jr. has it, too, and there are a couple of other suspected cases. Everyone around is flaming mad at the birds for contaminating us with their dirt. But me, I'm glad. Better histoplasmosis than a broken wishbone. And I think the disease has made it easier for Mom to go along with the tree-cutting.

The men have been at it all week and today they'll be through. I can watch from my bedroom window and it gives me something to do. The sound of the chain saw drowns out everything, even the thoughts I'm thinking. The trees come down with a terrible crash and the air is filled with a floating haze of sawdust. The sun turns the haze pink sometimes, or golden.

The men are wearing masks, like doctors about to operate, and the whole place had to be sprayed with disinfectant before they started.

Some of the trees have red crosses on them and they are the ones that are to be left standing. Dad told Mom we could keep ten, and they went out together and Mom touched the trees that were to be saved and Dad marked them using a can of spray paint. I watched them from my window, and I thought Mom was like an angel of God or something.

Mr. Dobbs was right. I can see Joe Jr.'s house now. He's getting better, too, because histoplasmosis is a bummer and it's slow, but it does respond well to antibiotics. That's another true thing Kelsey said. But we won't be tube-riding for what's left of the summer.

Fred Johnson spends a lot of time sleeping on my bed, curled up on the pillow. He loves the molasses cookies Mrs. Dobbs sent over. The crumbs are sticky and they cling to his whiskers.

I'm still stuttering, but the wishbone feels looser. I think it's because I can close my eyes and relive what I saw in the kitchen before I fell and for the first time I'm facing up to something. It's never going to be over. A fight past is only time bought till the next one comes along. The world is filled with traps for us. Seals, porpoises, hawks, insecticides. They'll never be able to change each other.

Once I asked Grandpa how he could stand it, not being able to walk any more.

"At first I was madder than hell," he said. "Then I learned to face facts. This is the way I'll always be. Now I make the best of what I've got and I'm thankful."

I've decided to make the best of what I've got too. I'm ready to talk to someone about it and I think it should be Dr. Green, because of the way his eyes were. I'm sure he's smart enough to have figured out my wishbone legs by now. If he hasn't, I'll draw him another picture with the new pastels Grandma sent. Anyway, I've decided that my wishbone's pretty strong and it can handle anything, as long as they don't give up.

Mom picked up my photographs from the drugstore. The bird picture was only a bunch of shadows. I'd planned on giving it to her so she could finish her painting, but maybe it's better not to remind her of the way the birds were. And how the maple trees used to look.

The strangest, strangest thing happened last night. I wakened, and I heard a bird singing outside in our trees. It was dark, dark as death, and I stumbled out of bed and felt my way to the window. I couldn't see a thing.

But somewhere outside in the blackness a single bird sang. Was it one that got left behind? Or one that had come back to mourn its friends who used to live here? Or was it a ghostbird singing in the dark of night?

It sang and it sang as if it thought that night was day, and I could still hear it as I drifted back to sleep.

I looked for it as soon as I wakened this morning but our ten trees with their red crosses stood silent and empty.